ISLINGTON LIBRARIES

3 0120 02105394 8

IGTON

The Silver Mirror

The Satin Dress
The Diamond Tiara
The Velvet Cloak
The Glass Slippers

The Silver Mirror
The Flowered Apron
The Pearly Comb
The Lace Gown

COMING SOON

Pearl's Dressing-up Dreams

The Silver
Mirror

JENNY OLDFIELD

Hodder
Children's
Books

A division of Hachette Children's Books

Text copyright © 2008 Jenny Oldfield
Illustrations © 2008 Artful Doodlers

First published in Great Britain in 2008
by Hodder Children's Books

The right of Jenny Oldfield to be identified as the author of this work
has been asserted by her in accordance with the
Copyright, Designs and Patents Act 1988.

1

All rights reserved. Apart from any use permitted under UK copyright
law, this publication may only be reproduced, stored or transmitted,
in any form, or by any means with prior permission in writing from
the publishers or in the case of reprographic production in accordance
with the terms of licences issued by the Copyright Licensing Agency
and may not be otherwise circulated in any form of binding or cover
other than that in which it is published and without a similar
condition being imposed on the subsequent purchaser.

All characters in this publication are fictitious and any resemblance
to real persons, living or dead, is purely coincidental.

A Catalogue record for this book is available from the British Library

ISBN-13: 978 0 340 95597 0

Printed and bound in Great Britain
by Clays Ltd, St Ives plc

The paper and board used in this paperback by Hodder Children's
Books are natural recyclable products made from wood grown in
sustainable forests. The manufacturing processes conform to the
environmental regulations of the country of origin.

ISLINGTON LIBRARIES	
3 0120 02195394 8 A	
PETERS	08-Aug-2008
£3.99	
F	

1

"I don't feel like dressing up today," Lily said.

"Tough," Pearl told her. "It's raining. Amber and I want to play in the basement, don't we, Amber?"

"Yep." Amber led the way down the steps.

"Don't go outside," her mother called to the girls from the kitchen. "You'll get wet."

Sighing, Lily followed Amber and Pearl.

She sat down on the bottom step and watched them open the lid of Amber's dressing-up box.

"What shall we wear today?" Pearl wondered, digging deep.

Out came Amber's shimmery Cinderella dress and some fairy wings, a witch's hat and a Superman cape. Amber and Pearl tossed them through the air and they landed on the floor.

"How do I look?" Pearl demanded, putting on the bright blue cape and flexing her muscles.

"What about this?" Amber tried on the wonky witch's hat. "It's Halloween – woo-woooo!"

"Don't just throw stuff on the floor!" Still sulking, Lily picked up Amber's fabulous fairy-tale frock. She held it up against herself and swished the soft skirt this way and that.

"Try it on," Amber suggested.

"No thanks." Lily was about to fold the dress neatly and put it back in the box when a heavy object banged against her leg. She slipped her hand into the skirt pocket and pulled out a silver mirror. "Where did this come from?"

"Woo-woo, witchy-woo!" Witch Amber glanced at the mirror. "Oh, yeah, I'd forgotten about that." She'd brought it back from Cinderella world on her last visit. "It was just there, in my pocket," she shrugged.

"It's mucky," Lily muttered.

The carved mirror was smeared with dirt

7

so Lily decided to give it a wipe.

She rubbed until her reflection was clear. "'Mirror, mirror, on the wall . . .'"

The mirror glinted back at her. Then there was a sudden flash of white light and with a whoosh, Lily was gone.

"Hey!" Pearl cried. "Lily, come back!"

"Uh-oh!" Amber muttered. "It's that magic thing. It's happening to Lily!"

Whoosh! Lily clung on to the mirror and floated on a white cloud. She turned and spun in midair until she was dizzy.

"Come back!" Pearl cried again.

"Good luck!" Amber yelled after Lily. "Enjoy the trip!"

"Whoa!" Lily landed with a thump. She opened her eyes and it was snowing.

Flakes fell softly to the ground. She was wrapped in a white fur cloak, still clutching the magic mirror tightly in her hand.

"Tut!" a voice said as a white horse with

a fine red leather saddle was led away. "Tut-tut, come inside, Princess, before you catch your death of cold."

Princess? This can't be Cinderella world, can it? Lily glanced around. Men in big leather boots, feathered caps and long capes were jumping from horses and striding through the snow towards a wide doorway. A stout old woman rushed towards her with an extra cloak.

"Wait a minute!" Lily exclaimed. "You've made a mistake. I'm not a prin—!"

Too late. She was smothered in more fur and velvet and whisked away.

Bang! The heavy doors closed shut behind her.

"Tut, my dove, give me that mirror," the old woman urged as she rushed Lily down a long corridor, up some narrow stone steps into a fancy bedchamber. "Where did you find it, my darling? Her Most Royal Highness was in a fury over losing it earlier today."

My dove? My darling? "It was in my pocket," Lily confessed. *What is this? What's happening?*

The old servant took off Lily's cloaks and shook the snow from them. She led her to a fire roaring in a wide grate. "Sit here and warm yourself while I slip the mirror back on its hook without Her MRH spotting me. Then all will be well."

"Will it?" Lily muttered to herself as the old woman huffed and puffed and dashed away.

She went to a narrow window and looked out at a snowy forest and mountains beyond. Lily felt like a small dot lost in a big white wilderness. "Amber, Pearl, where are you? I need help," she cried. "I haven't a clue where I am!"

"It is done." The stout old woman in the long green skirt and plain brown shawl bustled back. "Now come, my pigeon, we must get you ready for His Most Royal Highness's great feast this evening."

"B-b-but!" Lily protested.

A procession of young women in long, flowing dresses came into the room with warm water in a basin and perfumed soaps and towels. One carried a stiff white petticoat, another a shimmering gown. Yet another came with stockings and pretty satin shoes.

"No buts!" the old woman said firmly. "His MRH wishes you to sit at supper with him and the Queen, and all their guests."

A maid-servant took off Lily's blue velvet riding clothes and washed her arms and face. A second dabbed fragrant powder on her cheeks. Then a third held out the petticoat and Lily stepped into it.

"Everyone who is anyone will be there," the old servant explained. "The huntsmen who rode out into the forest with His Majesty have been invited to the feast. And of course, your very own handsome Prince Lovelace will be there."

"H-he will?" Lily stammered as another lady-in-waiting slipped a dress of silver and gold over her head. She breathed in as the woman laced her in. "Are you sure this isn't too small for me?" she gasped.

"See how the child blushes!" the old servant laughed. She gave Lily's cheek a quick pinch. "Don't act coy with me, Princess. Why, I've nursed you since you were an infant!"

Smiling and nodding, the ladies combed Lily's hair and smoothed out her shimmering folds. "Nurse knows you through and through," they murmured. "So save your blushes for the Prince!"

Whoa! Lily took a deep breath. She hadn't lifted a finger, yet here she was dressed in a stunning gown of gold and

silver cloth. Her feet were in satin slippers and her hair decorated with silver combs. She was all set to dine with a prince!

Then there was a knock at the door. "Her Most Royal Highness wishes to see the Princess before supper!" a snooty manservant announced.

"Tut!" The Nurse frowned and made the

maid-servants twirl Lily around. "Let me see – a little tweak here, a tug there – yes, you are ready!" she announced proudly.

"The Queen awaits you in her chamber," the manservant told Lily.

"Remember, my duckling, be on your best behaviour," her Nurse reminded her. "Smile and curtsey. Speak only when you're spoken to."

"OK!" Lily braced herself. The ladies-in-waiting seemed suddenly tense, which meant that this meeting with the Queen was a big thing.

"Let's hope Her MRH is in a good temper tonight," Nurse muttered, giving Lily's skirt one final tweak.

"Follow me, Your Royal Highness," the manservant said, walking stiffly ahead.

Lily felt her skirt trail behind her as she walked. Her heart beat rapidly against her tightly laced bodice.

This can't be happening! she thought as the manservant stopped outside a white and gold door.

He knocked twice with his silver stick and waited.

"Enter!" an impatient woman's voice called from within. "Don't dilly-dally out in the corridor. Snow White, I wish to speak to you. Come in at once!"

3

"Snow White," the Queen began. She paused to inspect Lily from head to toe.

Lily was too shocked to remember her manners. Could this be right? Had she really stepped into Snow-White world?

"My spies tell me that you went out riding in the forest today," the Queen continued.

Tongue-tied, Lily stared back. The

Queen was tall and young, with smooth dark hair. She was dressed in crimson velvet with a golden sash around her slinky hips to match her crown set with giant rubies. Red rings sparkled on her slim fingers.

"Speak, child," the Queen commanded. "What's the matter? Did the cat get your tongue?"

Lily nodded. "Yes. I mean, no. Yes!"

Her MRH looked down on Lily through hooded lids. Her top lip curled in scorn. "Did you or did you not leave the palace without my permission?"

"I did," Lily confessed. *Or at least, I guess I did, though I couldn't say for sure. My brain's in a muddle, and it doesn't help to have you glaring at me like that!*

20

"Disobedient girl!" the Queen screeched. "How many times must I tell you not to sneak off like that?"

"S-s-sorry!" Afraid that Queenie was about to explode, Lily backed away. "I won't do it again."

Her MRH took a deep breath. "Perhaps your mother used to let you roam like a beggar beyond the palace walls," she said snootily. "But now she is dead and I am Queen. You shall do as I say."

OK, I get the message! "Yes, Your Most Royal Highness."

"Nurse Gretchen shall answer to me for letting you ride out alone," the Queen muttered. "She shall be punished."

"Oh, I'm sure it wasn't her fault," Lily said quickly.

"Perhaps not, but she shall be punished anyway." For a long time the Queen kept her stern gaze on Lily. "Who chose that ugly dress?" she asked.

"I did!" Lily lied.

"And those ridiculous shoes?"

"Me!"

"And those nasty silver combs in your hair?"

"Me." *Guilty on all counts. No point getting anyone else into trouble*, Lily decided. "I thought I looked OK."

The Queen's lip curled until it almost touched her nose. "Go back to your room and change your dress," she ordered. "Put on the spotted yellow one with the purple sash which I bought for your birthday. Get Nurse to scrape back your hair and scrub

22

your face. Do you understand?"

"Got it," Lily mumbled as the Queen turned towards a small carved mirror hanging above her dressing table.

I recognise that mirror! Lily said to herself. She wished now she'd never taken it out of Amber's Cinderella pocket and rubbed it clean. *Look where being Little Miss Neat and Tidy got me!* she thought.

"Go now!" the Queen snapped, with her back to Lily.

As Lily crept from the room, she could see Her MRH staring into the mirror and she heard snatches of a rhyme. Not "Mirror, mirror . . .", but

"Tell me, glass, tell me true!
Of all the ladies in the land,
Who is the fairest? Tell me who?"

Lily didn't wait to hear the mirror's reply. Instead she closed the Queen's door and fled.

"Psst!"

As Lily ran down the corridor, Nurse Gretchen called.

"Psst! Snow White, come this way!" The old woman stepped out from behind a curtain and grabbed Lily by the arm. She

24

whisked her on to a gallery overlooking the main hall and hugged her tight.

"Oof!" Lily struggled free from sturdy Gretchen's embrace.

"Did the Queen hurt you? Why were you speeding away in such fright?" Gretchen demanded.

Lily fought off a second hug. "I'm OK, honestly! The Queen told me off for going riding then she ordered me to wear another dress, that's all. She said I have a purple spotted one."

"Tutttt-ttt! I knew it!" The Nurse frowned and spoke in a whisper. "I've said it before – you're much too pretty for the new Queen's liking, my dear, my dove."

In the hall below, servants carried great plates of meat and bread to the long table, which already groaned under the weight of the silver goblets and bowls piled high with apples, nuts and oranges.

Then the Queen swept into the hall dressed in her crimson gown with its long train, pointing at the table and finding fault wherever she looked. "Move this! . . . Polish that! . . . Bring more wine!"

"Stay back – don't let her see us!" the nervous Nurse warned Lily. "On my life, she would punish us most severely for lingering here!"

But it was too late – the eagle-eyed Queen had spotted a movement in the gallery. "Nurse Gretchen, I see you up there!" she shrieked. "Come down at once!"

The poor Nurse gasped. "Go!" she ordered Lily. "Before she sees you too."

So Lily turned and ran once more.

"What are you doing, you old fool?" The sound of Her Most Royal Highness's bossy voice scolding the Nurse followed Lily down the corridor. "I shall have you flung into the dungeon for lurking in the shadows . . . I shall have you starved and kept in the dark until you are sorry indeed!"

4

The corridors of the palace hummed with activity.

As Lily ran to change her frock, she bumped into a maid carrying a pile of crisp, clean sheets into her bedroom.

Rush – bump – "Oops!"

"Forgive me, Your Royal Highness!" the girl cried as the pile of sheets dropped to the floor and scattered. "Please don't tell the Queen, I beg of you!"

"No problem. It was totally my fault," Lily replied, helping her to pick up the linen.

Just then, a crowned figure appeared at the end of the corridor. He wore a tunic of white satin trimmed with ermine and a cloak of deep red velvet. As he came towards Lily, he smiled.

Uh-oh, here comes His MRH! Lily said to herself. *I hope he's not as nasty as Her!* She bowed her head and curtsied low.

"Snow White, how pretty you look!" King Jakob said, smiling and holding out his hand. "Are you ready for the feast?"

"Nearly," Lily answered. "The Queen says I have to get changed out of this dress."

"Nonsense!" the King argued, looking his daughter up and down. "You are perfect as you are."

"B-but . . ." Lily dreaded what Queenie would say if Snow White turned up in her gold and silver gown.

King Jakob held Lily by the hand. "You

must not change a thing," he insisted gently. "Come with me now and greet our guests."

So the King and Lily went down the broad stairs arm in arm. She heard the sound of sleigh bells jingling in the courtyard and the blare of silver trumpets announcing the arrival of Lord This and Lady That, the Duke and Duchess of So-and-So, the Prince of the Green Forest and the Queen of Ice Mountain.

"Wow!" Lily gasped.

The wide doors opened on to a white wonderland. Out in the courtyard, black horses drew silver sleighs through the palace gates. They pranced proudly with silver plumes on their heads and bells on their harnesses.

"Pretty!" Lily gasped and clapped her hands together.

The sleighs stopped and footmen opened doors to let the lords and ladies step out.

"Cool!" Lily murmured.

A girl with a golden plait hanging to her waist wore a gown of midnight blue with a sash of silver. Her hands were hidden inside a white fur muff.

Marks out of ten – eight and a half!

"Next!" she muttered as another sleigh door opened.

Out stepped a young man. His dark hair was cut in a chin-length bob and he wore a tunic of soft black leather studded with silver. A sword swung at his waist.

Seven out of ten. Shame about the haircut!

Suddenly Lily was having a good time, standing beside King Jakob on a red carpet, smiling and curtseying.

Next to bow down low was an old man in a brown fur cape with gold chains around his neck. Then his wife and daughter, frouffing their frills and putting on their smiles.

A three, a four and a five.

Lily was getting good at this. At home she read her mum's gossip mags – she knew which fashions she liked and those she didn't.

"Ah, Prince Lovelace!" King Jakob stepped forward to greet the latest arrival.

Pay attention! Lily thought, dragging her gaze away from some splendid white horses. *This is the one the Nurse talked about.*

The Prince bowed low. A diamond badge sparkled in his black feathered cap. His tunic was royal purple, his boots supple and black.

"Your Most Royal Highness!" Prince Lovelace spluttered.

He looked up and Lily gasped aloud, but

this time not in delight.

The Prince was a chinless wonder with staring eyes and a bent nose. His wispy brown hair straggled over thin cheeks.

The King shook him by the hand. "So good of you to come, my boy. How did you enjoy today's sport?"

"Superb!" Prince Lovelace piped. "A perfect day of sport, Your Most Royal Highness!"

Minus five out of ten! Lily groaned. *What a geek! What a total let-down – my very own handsome prince!*

5

B-o-r-ing!

For a whole hour Lily had sat next to the chinless wonder.

"A splendid supper after a superb day's sport! . . . Your Most Royal Father, the King is so generous and kind to invite me . . . Her Majesty the Queen is so beautiful . . . so kind!"

Lily yawned. How come she had to sit

next to the geekiest person here? Why not the girl with the golden plait, or the cute boy with the bad haircut?

Further down the table, the King and Queen held court.

"Serena, my dear, my royal brother, the Prince of the Green Forest, is an excellent shot," King Jakob was telling his wife. "Today he was even more skilled than usual."

The Prince shook his head at the compliment. "Not nearly so good a shot as your Most Royal Highness," he replied.

B-o-ring!! Lily hid another yawn.

"May I say how perfectly lovely the royal Princess looks tonight," the Queen of Ice Mountain leaned across the table to tell the King and Queen.

"Indeed!" King Jakob agreed, smiling down the table and catching Lily's eye.

Queen Serena gave a little sniff. "Really, Your Ice Majesty? Do you think her dress is quite right for the occasion?"

"Why, yes!" the kindly Queen replied. Then, as she saw Serena frown, "Well, perhaps not . . ." Then, noticing King Jakob's sharp look in her direction, "Yes, yes – Snow White's dress is perfect!"

Queen Serena suddenly stood up and ordered the dancing to begin. As the musicians began to play, she strode towards Lily.

Whoops! Lily sat tight as Her MRH descended. *What now?*

"Snow White, why didn't you change into your purple spotted dress?" Serena

38

stooped to hiss in her ear.

"I didn't . . . I couldn't . . ." Lily stammered. But she could tell the Queen was in no mood for excuses.

"Go upstairs now and put it on!" Serena insisted, her eyes darting daggers. Then she stood up straight and fake-smiled at Prince Lovelace, who jumped to his feet.

"Would Your Most Royal Highness do me the honour of joining me in the first dance?" he asked.

So, while the Queen and her Prince waltzed, off Lily went to find her purple shock-frock.

She searched through the many fine silk and satin dresses hanging in her wardrobe until she came to the bright spotted number.

"Yuck!" Lily said as she pulled it off the rail. "I'll look like a clown in this!"

But no way did she dare to defy Queenie. Quickly she called Gretchen to loosen her laces and help her change into the ugly duckling outfit.

"I've a good mind to speak out and tell the King what his bad-tempered wife is up to!" the Nurse grumbled. "It's plain as the nose on my face that the wicked woman is jealous of you, my little chick!"

With the cotton frock laced up tight, Lily snuck a look in the mirror. She was swamped by lilac frills and purple spots. "Gross!" she groaned.

But she had to go back to the feast dressed like this, or else!

"Poor dove, poor duckling!" Nurse

Gretchen cooed after her. "Whatever will Prince Lovelace think!"

I don't care if it puts Pester-Face off! Lily thought as she hurried past the Queen's chamber in her frilly fright. *Actually, that would be one good thing!*

But Lily wasn't the only one who had slipped away from the party. Queen Serena was in her room, chatting to her mirror.

"Tell me, glass, tell me true!

Of all the ladies in the land,

Who is the fairest? Tell me who?"

Lily paused and was about to tiptoe past the door. But this time she longed to know if the mirror would reply.

"Tell me, glass, tell me true!" the Queen repeated.

Lily peered into the room to see Serena preening herself in front of the mirror, turning this way and that to catch her best side.

"Of all the ladies in the land,

Who is the fairest? Tell me who?"

The shiny mirror glinted then answered in a slow, whispering voice, "Thou, Queen, art fairest in the land."

Queen Serena took a deep breath then smiled. "Thank you!" she whispered back to the mirror, with Lily looking on. "My silvery friend, thank you indeed!"

6

"How well I recall the days when your mother was alive," Gretchen murmured as she brushed Lily's hair.

The feast had ended and Lily was getting ready for bed. Her purple frock lay crumpled on the floor.

"We were happy then. Your mother laughed and sang as she went about the palace and you, my chicken, toddled after.

She was the sweetest lady with the kindest heart, and everyone loved her."

Lily sighed and buttoned up her nightgown. It made her sad to think how much things had changed for the people at the palace.

"You were her joy," the Nurse confided, as Lily laid her head on the soft pillow. "Before you were born, I would hear her kneel by her bed each night and pray for a daughter with skin as white as snow and cheeks as red as blood. She was the happiest woman alive when she got her wish!"

"I don't remember," she whispered. "But it sounds lovely."

Gretchen patted her hand. "You were the most beautiful infant. Never a mark on your pure skin, and hands so tiny and perfectly formed! And a lively, spirited thing, tottering on your own feet before you were twelve months old, poking into this and that, driving us to distraction!"

Lily smiled. The wind lifted the curtains at the narrow window.

Then the Nurse sighed. "Little did we know how soon it was to alter."

Out in the corridor, a door banged. Footsteps sounded in the distance.

"But hush!" Gretchen said with another heavy sigh. "We must not talk too loudly about the old days."

"Why not?"

"Her Most Royal Highness has forbidden it," the Nurse explained, tucking Lily in one last time. Then she pulled the drapes straight and prepared to leave.

"Goodnight, my little wren," she whispered. "And remember that times have changed."

"Totally," Lily agreed. *And how!*

Nurse Gretchen nodded sadly. "These days, there are spies round every corner. Even the walls have ears!"

Next day, Lily woke early to blue skies and the sound of voices in the courtyard below.

"Fetch Her Most Royal Highness's horse immediately!"

"Her Most Royal Highness will join the hunt today!"

"Hurry! The Queen is coming!"

Lily got out of bed and looked down on the scene. She saw grooms running to the stables to saddle Serena's horse while other servants swept the courtyard clear of fallen snow. Six or seven riders in short cloaks and feathered hats were already in the saddle, including the King himself and geeky Prince Pester-Face.

Yippee, we can relax! Lily realised that the Queen would be out for the day. "Maybe I can get some more stories out of old Gretchen and then start thinking about how I'm going to get out of here!"

"Here comes Her Most Royal Highness!" a servant called, and Queen Serena made her grand entrance into the courtyard.

Wrapped from top to toe in a sable cloak, she swept into view. On her head she wore a lavish black fur hat. Her gloves and boots were of soft black Spanish leather, her spurs were pure silver.

"Greetings, gentlemen!" she said in her haughtiest voice. "What shall we hunt today? Shall it be the antlered stag or the silver fox?"

"The stag!" Prince Lovelace cried, while the Prince of the Green Forest hid his smiles behind his gauntlet.

"Then let it be the stag, for you and me, Prince Lovelace. And let my husband, the

King, and the Prince of the Green Forest, chase the silver fox." Handing out the orders as usual, the Queen mounted her black horse and joined the geek.

"As you wish," King Jakob replied, wheeling his chestnut horse around and leading the Prince and lords of his party out through the palace gates.

OK, she might be good-looking, but she is one serious bully! Lily watched the Queen and Pester-Face ride off in the opposite direction. Then she picked up the silver bell on her bedside table. "Nurse!" she called with a ring of the bell.

She rang three times before anyone appeared.

"May I be of assistance, Your Royal Highness?" a lady-in-waiting asked.

"I was ringing for Gretchen," Lily explained. "I was hoping she'd help me decide what to wear today."

"Nurse Gretchen cannot come," the girl said hastily.

"Oh." Lily frowned. She liked the Nurse, she decided, even if she was too free with the bird-words. *Little dove, little duckling.* "What's wrong? Why can't she come?"

"I am not permitted to say, Your Royal Highness," the girl replied, without looking Lily in the eye. "May I suggest your gown of embroidered satin?"

"Hm." Lily had stopped listening. She wanted to know what had happened to her Nurse, full-stop. "Is she ill? She was OK last night – fit as a fiddle, in fact."

"Or the gown of green velvet with the

pearl buttons?" the girl went on.

"Wait here," Lily said hurriedly. She brushed past the lady-in-waiting and went out into the corridor. "Gretchen, where are you?" she called loudly.

Then other women came running up the stairs, armed with petticoats and stockings, brushes, ribbons and jewels. They bustled Lily back into her chamber and dressed her in her princess finery.

"OK, enough!" Lily said at last. "You can go now."

The ladies curtsied and backed away. "Yes, Your Royal Highness. Does Your Royal Highness wish for anything else? Anything at all?"

"No!" Lily said firmly. What she wished for was to get rid of them so that she could go and find the Nurse.

So as soon as the door was closed and peace descended on the palace, Lily left her room and began her search.

"Nurse?" she called along the corridor and into each room she passed.

There was no answer.

She went downstairs to the great hall, along the narrow wooden gallery. "Nurse Gretchen, where are you?"

Once, a door opened, then hastily closed. A servant boy with dark spiky hair and ragged breeches scuttled by carrying an iron kitchen pot. "Hey!" Lily called after him, but he didn't stop.

"Gretchen!" Lily shouted for her friend in the hall and then in the vast, empty kitchen where rows of pans hung from hooks and a fire was laid under a giant cauldron. Here she spied the potboy a second time. "Hey!" she cried again.

Shyly the boy emerged from a shadowy corner. He bowed stiffly.

Lily saw that he was trembling. "It's OK, don't be scared," she told him. "I'm not really Snow . . . Oh, forget it! Anyway, I'm not vicious and nasty like Her Most Royal You-know-who!"

The potboy gasped and stared.

"Listen," Lily went on. "I'm trying to find Gretchen. Have you seen her?"

Rapidly the boy shook his head. His knees knocked together and his teeth chattered.

"Wow, you really are scared!" Lily muttered. Then she remembered what her

Nurse had said about the walls having ears. "Listen, if you can't say anything, just nod or shake your head, OK?"

Darting rapid glances around the kitchen, the boy nodded.

"I'm guessing, but I think you know where Gretchen is, don't you?" Lily hissed.

He nodded.

"Is she OK?"

He shook his head.

Lily's heart missed a beat. "Is she sick?"

Another shake of the head.

"Is she – dead?"

Shake, shake.

Phew! "Is this something to do with the Queen?" Lily asked.

The boy nodded.

By now, Lily was stuck and it was the potboy who made the next move. Looking around carefully once more, he plucked up the courage to take Lily by the hand and lead her to a small door at the far side of the kitchen.

"You want me to open it?" she asked.

He nodded then stood to one side.

So Lily did as he said and opened the heavy door on to a long, dark, narrow passage. "Is Gretchen down here?"

The potboy nodded.

"Thanks!" Lily told him swiftly, before he scuttled off like a frightened mouse escaping from the cat's sharp claws.

This was it, then – a dark passageway with no lights but plenty of cobwebs. Lily took a few steps forward.

Flit-flit-flit! A bat flew by, brushing her hair.

"Ewww! This is like the Ghost Train at the fair, only for real!" Lily gritted her teeth, stepping through puddles and under dripping arches until she came to a dimly lit square chamber with three doors which were barred and bolted. The palace dungeons!

"Serena wouldn't!" Lily gasped.

"Who's there?" a muffled voice asked from inside one of the cells. "Princess, my dove, is that you?"

7

"I did warn you about our precious Queen," Gretchen reminded Lily.

Through the bars of the cell Lily made out the huddled shape of the old Nurse. "But I didn't think she'd do this. She can't just lock people up for no reason!"

"But she can," Gretchen insisted. "As you plainly see."

"What for?" Lily wanted to know, trying

to imagine what it must be like to be thrown into this black hole and hearing the key turn in the lock. Then the silence, except for the drip-drip-drip of the water trickling from the arches and the flit-flit of bats' wings brushing against the walls.

"According to Her Most Royal Highness, I am a spy!" Gretchen explained. "She says I poison your mind with wicked stories and untruths, that I am a traitor and that I deserve to die."

Lily was alarmed. "But you can deny it! You will have a trial and you can tell the truth. It's the Queen who is wicked!"

"There will be no trial," the Nurse told Lily bleakly. "I will be locked up in this dungeon and people will forget about me."

"Not me!" Lily promised boldly.

"In the end, everyone will forget, including you, my precious," Gretchen insisted sadly. "You are young, with your whole life ahead of you."

Lily reached through the bars to grasp her Nurse's hand. "I'll tell the King the truth!" she swore. "He'll listen to me and he'll let you out."

"Take care, my lark," Gretchen begged. "Do not make things worse."

"I'll find the King!" Lily clenched her fist. "He's out hunting in the forest, but I'll follow him and explain what's happened. I'll be back before midday, I promise!"

Gretchen grasped the cell bars and pressed her face to the gaps. "Be careful!" she pleaded. "Do not cross the Queen, I beg of you!"

But Lily was gone, running back the way she had come, along the dismal passage into the kitchen and out into the courtyard and the glaring winter sun.

Lily found the palace empty and silent as before. There were no grooms to saddle a horse for her or servants to open the gates out on to the vast forest.

"Where is everyone?" she muttered,

rushing into the stables and luckily finding a grey horse saddled and bridled, ready to ride.

"Steady," Lily told the mare, leading her gingerly out of her stable.

The horse twitched her ears and tossed her head.

"Listen," Lily explained quickly. "It's like this. Me and horses – well, I've never had any riding lessons. In fact, right now I'm pretty scared of you!"

The mare listened and stamped a front hoof. Then she lowered her head to nudge Lily's hand.

"You seem nice, but I don't even know if I can ride you!" Lily went on breathlessly. "Anyway, this is important. I have to find King Jakob and get him to free my Nurse

from the dungeons, because she hasn't done a single thing wrong except say what everyone else knows about the Queen but is too scared to admit . . ."

The grey horse stood patiently, as if understanding every word. Then she turned her head as if to say, *Please stop jabbering and get up in the saddle so we can set off!*

So Lily put her foot in the stirrup and clumsily swung into the saddle. *Now what? Do I click my tongue and say "Giddy-up"?*

The wise horse definitely had a mind of her own and seemed to know what Lily wanted. She set off slowly at first, across the courtyard and out into the trees beyond. Then she began to pick up pace.

"Whoa!" Lily breathed, clinging tight.

The mare slowed and waited for her to settle into the saddle. *Ready?*

"Yeah, OK, I've got my balance," Lily muttered. "Now trot!"

And the horse set off at a smart pace, following a trail in the snow which led between the tall fir trees, deeper and deeper into the forest.

Up-down, up-down! Lily joggled in the

saddle until she got the hang of the horse's rhythm.

The trail led where the sun no longer shone through the branches and clumps of soft snow fell to earth with a thud.

"Scary!" Lily muttered, looking up at the snow-laden branches. But she kept poor Gretchen in mind and rode on.

Ta-ra-ta-ra-ta-taaa! A huntsman blew his trumpet and a creature broke through the undergrowth into the clearing. It was a stag with huge antlers, crashing past Lily and her horse. Behind him, hounds cried and huntsmen blew their horns.

Poor thing, I hope they don't catch him! Lily shuddered and urged her horse on, away from the sound of the hounds.

The mare tossed her head and walked forward along a narrow trail.

"I hope you know where you're going!" Lily muttered, surprised to see a small cottage and woodshed ahead in another clearing, surrounded by a sturdy fence. *Who would live here?* she wondered. *Right in the middle of the forest!*

But there was no time to stop and look,

though Lily could squint inside the house and see a long table set for supper. Five – six – seven chairs and seven places, all neatly arranged, ready for the owners' return. "Cosy!" Lily said.

But then the huntsmen's horns sounded again, closer, and riders came into view.

"Stop!" a voice cried.

"Stop, stranger, or prepare to die!"

Prince Lovelace called.

"Oh no, just what I need!" Lily groaned, pulling her horse to a halt.

She waited for the Prince to ride up, closely followed by the Queen and two huntsmen.

"Why, Princess!" Lovelace exclaimed as he drew near and recognised Lily. "Whatever are you doing here?"

"Step aside!" Queen Serena ordered the Prince before Lily had time to answer. She rode up in her black fur cloak, her face under her fur hat set in an angry mask. "Ah, I see it is the wayward Snow White, disobeying orders once more!"

Lily pursed her lips. She tried to outstare the Queen, but Serena's fierce, cruel gaze scared her and she looked away.

"Well, we must find a punishment for you," Her Most Royal Highness decided.

"Like the one you found for Gretchen?" Lily answered back.

"Hah!" The Queen's tone changed to mockery. "I see you have turned spy too, my dear stepdaughter. You have discovered the fate of your Nurse!"

Lily tried to disguise her trembling hands. She drew herself up tall in the saddle. "I'm going to find the King and tell him what you've done!"

"Ha-ha!" Throwing back her head, Queen Serena laughed long and hard. "You little fool! You think you can cross me, but you are mistaken!"

"OK, so laugh!" Lily retorted, turning her horse away and riding on. She thought she could hear yet more horns close by and the sound of galloping hooves. Soon new riders broke through the trees – huntsmen riding hard, kicking up snow as they went. When they saw Snow White, they reined around and rode towards her, the King at their head.

"Daughter, I am amazed!" King Jakob began. "I thought we had left you asleep in your warm bed!"

"You did. I was," Lily admitted, stumbling over her words. "But I need to talk to you. It's important!"

"Slow down, my dear," the King said, worried. "What can be the matter?"

"Why, nothing!" the Queen interrupted, riding between Lily and the King. "Snow White should not be out in the forest in these thin clothes. She must go back to the palace at once."

"Yes, yes," King Jakob agreed. He turned to Prince Lovelace. "Be so kind as to ride back with my daughter."

"No, not yet!" Lily cried. "I just found out that Gretchen is locked in the dungeons. I want you to set her free!"

"Gretchen, your old Nurse?" he asked with a puzzled frown. "Are you sure?"

Lily nodded. "Ask her!" she said, pointing to Queen Cruella.

"Is this true, Serena?" King Jakob asked in astonishment.

Straight away the Queen put on a special smile. Her voice turned sugary sweet. "Why, there must be some mistake," she cooed. "Snow White, were

you having a bad dream? Are you sure the faithful Nurse is where you say she is?"

"Totally!" Lily said. "I saw her."

"Then there has definitely been an error," the Queen said smoothly, turning to one of her huntsmen – a sallow man with a thin face and pointed beard. "Sir Manfred, please be so good as to ride ahead to the palace and order the release of Nurse Gretchen!"

"Quite right," King Jakob added,

smiling kindly at Lily. "You see, my dear, there is no need to worry."

If only you knew! Lily thought.

"Go!" Queen Serena said to her man through gritted teeth. Then the smile came back. "And now, Prince Lovelace, you can take Snow White home."

"Yes, make haste," the King said, squeezing Lily's hand. "You are frozen," he told her. "Such a dear, dear child to worry about poor Gretchen. Now you must go home and tell her all is well."

8

"And so you see, my dove, that we must never trust a single word the Queen says!" Newly freed from the dungeons, the Nurse sat by the fire in Lily's chamber. She thrust her icy feet into the bowl of hot water which Lily had brought.

"Mind you don't get chilblains," Lily told her. "Mum always says you shouldn't warm your feet up too fast."

"Ah, your poor mother!" Gretchen sighed. She shook her head sadly. "You know we are in grave danger?"

Lily nodded. "The Queen has seriously scary eyes," she murmured. "I don't understand – I mean, why doesn't the King get it too?"

The Nurse groaned as her feet entered the water. "Men are blind when they are in love," she explained. "Ooh – aah! Then, when Cupid's blindfold falls away, it is too late."

"So King Jakob's trapped?"

"In a marriage to a cruel, jealous Queen," Gretchen added. "And we must all suffer her rages and live in fear."

"That's so not fair!" Lily protested.

But the Nurse raised a warning finger.

"Hush! Listen!" she said.

"What? I can't hear anything." Except the wind blowing down the chimney and servants bustling in the courtyard below.

Then there were footsteps and a firm knock at the door.

"Enter!" Gretchen called.

A footman in deep red velvet came in. "His Most Royal Highness is home from the hunt," he reported. "He wishes to know if Her Royal Highness, Princess Snow White, returned safely to the palace."

"Tell him yes," Lily replied. "I'm fine, thanks." In spite of the earache she'd got from Prince Lovelace all the way back – "Your Royal Highness must be freezing! Please take my cloak. Let me shelter you from the snow!"

"Then His Most Royal Highness wishes Her Royal Highness, the Princess, to join him by the fire in the great hall, where they can talk privately."

Lily nodded. "Will you be OK if I leave you for a bit?" she asked Gretchen.

"Yes, you must go to your father, my little wren." Lifting her feet from the basin, Gretchen stood up. "But first, let me see how you look."

"Well?" Lily asked, doing a twirl. Luckily she'd chosen to wear a fine new gown. It was made of cream brocade, decorated down the front in green and red, with rows of tiny pearls and a long, embroidered train trailing behind.

The old Nurse clasped her hands

together. "I cannot believe my eyes!" she declared. "You are as bright as the day, and fairer than the Queen herself!"

"Sshh!" Lily warned.

The footman stood at the door. His eyelids flickered but he said nothing.

Nurse Gretchen bit her lip then she gushed some more. "In any case, I never saw such a perfect sight as you, my darling child!"

"His Most Royal Highness awaits!" the servant reminded Lily and Gretchen stiffly.

"Go!" the Nurse said, turning Lily towards the door with a gentle push.

I hope the King isn't mad with me, Lily thought as she hurried down the corridor.

Maybe Queenie got at him and blamed me for being out in the forest!

But Serena was in her own chamber when Lily passed. She was at her mirror as usual.

"Tell me, glass, oh tell me true!"

Lily paused by the door. *Not again!* Did the vain woman spend *all* her time looking at herself?

"Of all the ladies in the land,

Who is the fairest? Tell me who?"

Though she was in a hurry to join her father, something told Lily to wait for the magic mirror's answer. She held her breath and listened.

"Thou, Queen, may'st fair and beauteous be," the mirror replied.

Queen Serena's expression darkened

and she glowered at her reflection.
Her eyes narrowed and fury sparked
from them.

"Thou, Queen, may'st fair
and beauteous be,
But Snow White is lovelier
far than thee!"

9

"Be very afraid!" Lily told herself as she rushed on down the corridor.

The Queen burst out of her chamber and spied Lily. "Snow White, come back here!" she screeched, her face purple with fury. She stamped her feet and made the metal shields hanging from the walls shake and rattle.

Lily clenched her teeth and stopped on

the brink of the stone steps leading down to the great hall.

Serena stormed after her. "You treacherous girl!" she screamed.

"Why, what did I do?" Lily demanded. This time she was determined to stand up to the mad Queen. "I didn't do anything, except just be here!"

"Silence!" Her Most Royal Highness thundered while the footman quaked. Then she lowered her voice to a poisonous whisper. "I know your cunning plan! It is to take my place in the King's affections."

"No way!" Lily protested. *Actually, my cunning plan is to get out of here the second I find out how!*

The Queen gripped Lily's wrist hard. "There is no room in the King's heart for two people!" she hissed. "It is either you, Snow White, or it is me!"

"Who told you that?" Lily began. Thinking straight had always been something she was good at. "It doesn't work that way."

"Be silent!"

"No, you listen to me. Being part of this family isn't a Miss World competition, you know. Just because some magic mirror tells you you're not the fairest . . ."

"Aagh!" Unable to bear the truth, Serena hissed like a snake. She tried to shove Lily against the wall. "Traitor!"

"You're mad!" Lily retorted, twisting free and running down the stairs. "Completely crazy. I'm not even going to talk to you!"

*

Downstairs the fire was blazing and the King sat in a carved oak armchair. His face lit up when he saw Lily.

"I was worried about you this morning, my dear," he said, making room by the fire and patting the chair opposite.

"No need," Lily told him. "I like being out in the snow!"

King Jakob gazed at her, watching the firelight flicker across her pale face and

83

dark, sparkling eyes. "You are a free spirit, Snow White, just like your mother."

She smiled back at him. He had a kind face, with light grey eyes, a straight nose and a square chin. He definitely didn't deserve the Snake Wife.

"The snow falls hard at this time of year," King Jakob went on. "It is easy to get lost in the forest if you ride alone."

"I won't do it again," Lily promised.

"And how is Gretchen, your Nurse, after her stay in the dungeons?"

"She's upset. And cold. But I think she'll be OK." With a quick glance up the stairs, Lily was relieved to see that Serena hadn't followed her. Then she took a risk. "Gretchen's sure it was the Queen who had her thrown in there," she whispered.

King Jakob shook his head. "It was a mistake," he insisted. "And all ends well. Now, Snow White, we will while away the afternoon over a game of chess. How does that sound to you?"

"OK, so how did King Jakob get checkmate on my King?" Lily muttered as she went back up the stairs. "I noticed his Bishop but not his Knight."

"Better luck next time," the King had told her as he folded away the chequered board. "Now I must return to my guests, and you must get ready for supper."

Lily hurried past the Queen's chamber and into her own room. "Are you there, Gretchen?" she called.

Slowly the Nurse came out of an inner chamber, her stout body trembling.

"What's wrong? Are you ill?" Lily asked in alarm.

"No, no, it's just aches and pains, my dove." The Nurse swayed and had to hold on to a chair to steady herself. "Don't you worry your pretty head about me."

Lily rushed towards her. "You'd better sit down. I'll fetch you a glass of water."

Gratefully the old woman sat in the

chair. "Ah, my old bones," she sighed.

"Is it because the Queen put you in the dungeons?" Lily demanded.

Gretchen shook her head. She still seemed breathless. "It's nothing."

"Tell me!" Lily insisted

At which the old woman raised her coarse apron to her face and fell into a flood of tears. "Oh my lark!" she cried. "While you were away, I heard the most dreadful thing, which I swore not to tell you because it was so terrible, but which I cannot keep hidden from you, for it puts you in great danger, my dove!"

"What?" Lily cried, her heart

beating rapidly. "Slow down, Nurse. Try to explain."

"But then again, what good will it do?" the old woman wailed, rocking back and forth in her chair. "It will only give you nightmares. No, no, I must not tell!"

"Yes, you must," Lily said firmly. She pulled the Nurse's apron away from her face. "Dry your tears. Is it something to do with the Queen?"

"Oh, wicked!" Gretchen sobbed. "I have never seen her so angry, like a fierce tigress – and with you, my precious robin!"

Lily's heart skipped a beat. "Tell me," she urged.

"I passed by her chamber and heard voices," Gretchen explained. "She was talking with one of the huntsmen – Sir

Manfred, I suppose it was."

"And?" Lily prompted.

"Oh, the words I heard her say!" Once more Gretchen fell into loud sobs. "She has an evil heart – she says you are her enemy and means to see you no more!"

Lily took a deep breath. "How does she plan to make that happen?"

The Nurse wailed even more loudly than before. "She has told Sir Manfred to take you deep into the forest and to kill you. But he must make it look like a hunting accident, and so the King will be deceived!"

"Oh!" A chill ran through Lily. "Who's Sir Manfred? Is he the one with the thin face and pointy beard?"

Gretchen nodded. "He keeps close to the Queen's side and follows her every command in order to gain favour. In return for this evil deed she has promised to make him lord of a land beyond the mountains."

"So he'll do it?" Lily asked, shivering once more.

"I fear he will," the Nurse answered, breaking down once more. "Oh, my darling child, whatever shall we do?"

10

There was a friend beyond the forest, Nurse Gretchen told Lily.

"It is the Queen of Ice Mountain, sister to your dear mother. She was at the feast last night, but left for home before dawn this morning. You must flee this palace and ride to her without delay."

"Are you sure she'll help?" Lily asked.

"Trust me, she will be good to you,"

Gretchen promised. "She always loved her sister, and you are her only niece."

Lily nodded. "Maybe eventually she'll be able to talk some sense into King Jakob," she decided. "But I'll have to leave in secret, without Her Most Royal Highness getting to hear about it."

"And I will miss you, my dove," the Nurse cried. "It will tear my heart in two."

Lily hugged her and begged her not to cry. "It had better be tonight."

"Oh!" Gretchen sobbed. "But you will need a good horse to take you through the forest. And I know of no mount which will find its way at night."

Lily thought hard. "I don't want to hang around and let this Manfred grab me, so I need to leave while he's at supper, which is soon. But I won't ride through the forest in the dark. I'll hide nearby and set off at dawn. That way we won't get lost."

Gretchen listened then nodded. "You will need your fur cloak and boots. I will saddle the horse myself!"

"Choose the grey mare," Lily told her, letting the old woman rush down to the stables as she got dressed.

Then she tiptoed after her, along the corridor past Queen Serena's closed door, down the stairs and out through the grand entrance to the palace.

"Why, Princess!" Prince Lovelace exclaimed as he crossed the courtyard in the frosty night air. "What are you doing outside in the cold?"

"My horse is sick. I'm going to visit her,"

Lily answered him quickly.

The Prince bowed and scraped. "So kind!" he murmured. "So soft-hearted!"

"I must hurry," Lily told him. "But I will see you at supper, Prince Lovelace."

Satisfied, her Prince strode on into the

palace, while Lily hurried into the stables.

"And so, my dear, we must say farewell," the faithful Nurse told her as she handed over the grey mare's reins. There were no more sobs and tears, only a deep sadness in the old woman's eyes.

"But not for ever," Lily promised as she climbed into the saddle.

Gretchen raised her arm and held Lily's hand tight. "Who knows what the future may hold?" she whispered. "Only, keep yourself safe, my dearest, and seek refuge with the Queen of Ice Mountain, who is as different from this evil queen as chalk is from cheese, or winter is from summer."

"I will," Lily promised. "Goodbye, Gretchen."

"Goodbye, my dove," the Nurse replied

softly, staring into the darkness until long after Lily had ridden away.

"Walk on!" Lily told the grey horse.

The forest soon swallowed them. Trees stood tall and dark, their snowy branches bent close to the ground.

How far shall I ride? Lily wondered in the silence. *How soon will we be safely hidden?*

Her horse plodded on, knee-deep in

snow. She seemed to pick up a trail invisible to Lily but known by her – perhaps used by the huntsmen when they rode out after deer.

"Let's go off the trail," Lily said quietly, tugging at the reins and steering her between trees. "Not far, but just far enough."

This was in case Sir Manfred tried to follow her once they found out she was missing. Or perhaps her father would send out a search party in the middle of the night and have her brought home.

"We could find the clearing with the little cottage," Lily said hopefully. "Then I'd hide in the woodshed and keep warm."

So her horse walked on and more snow began to fall and there was total silence.

*

Was it Lily's imagination, or was her horse walking in circles?

Was that a glimpse of light between the trees, and were they sounds from the palace?

She pulled at the reins and stopped.

Yes, it was a light! Straight ahead, twinkling between the tree branches.

But no, those weren't palace noises – they were branches shedding snow as someone brushed clumsily by, they were the heavy breathing of a horse in hot pursuit and the low cursing of its rider.

"We're being followed!" Lily gasped, not knowing which way to turn.

"Walk on!" a man's voice growled at his horse. "Or do you wish to feel the sting of my spurs?"

Lily tucked her own horse behind a thick tree trunk. She held her breath.

"The Queen will punish me if I return empty-handed," the gruff, angry voice continued. "She hates Snow White and wants her dead. Well, the child will freeze to death out in the forest at night, so Her Most Royal Highness will get her wish!"

So this was Sir Manfred, Lily decided. How come he was so quick?

"And so will I freeze at this rate," Manfred muttered as his horse drew closer to Lily's hiding place. "Prince Lovelace be hanged, for it was he who told the mistrustful Queen that he had seen Snow White wrapped up in her fur cloak, visiting her sick horse in the stable. The fool set up a hue and cry."

Lily closed her eyes and hoped that her pursuer would ride on by.

"Snow White has left no trail!" Manfred cursed the falling snow. "How can I or anyone follow in this blizzard?"

Then his dark horse stopped dead.

For one heart-stopping moment Lily feared that Manfred's horse had picked up their scent and would lead his rider towards them. She pressed closer to the tree trunk.

"Walk on, you idle beast!" Manfred swore at his mount and kicked him roughly. He rode close to the tree where Lily hid. "Enough!" he growled, reining the gelding around and returning the way they had come. "The storm grows worse."

"Thank goodness!" Lily breathed again.

"I will tell Her Most Royal Highness that Snow White is dead," Manfred decided. "When the snow stops falling she may ride into the forest and find her body buried in a coffin of snow and ice!"

And with a hollow laugh, he rode away.

11

"I'll follow the light," Lily decided.

She waited until Manfred and his dark horse had vanished into the darkness then she urged the grey mare on towards the twinkling yellow light.

The horse trod softly through deep snow until they came to a clearing, and sure enough it was a light from the cottage with the sturdy fence.

"That's it – we'll hide here," she said, sliding from the saddle and choosing a tree behind the woodshed to tether her mare. "I hope you've got enough shelter," she whispered. "At least you're out of the wind. Wait here while I see if I can find anything for you to eat – maybe carrots or an apple."

Though the cottage seemed empty, Lily took care not to make any noise as she crept towards the nearest window and peered inside.

The curtains were open. No fire blazed in the hearth.

"The people who live here aren't home yet," Lily thought out loud. "Perhaps I can risk a quick look inside!"

So she stepped silently to the door

and tried the latch. It clicked and the door opened.

Lily noticed the seven plates set out on the long table, the seven chairs drawn up under it. "Hm."

A wind blew the door closed behind her. She tiptoed forward. "Is anyone home?"

Mysteriously the same wind opened a door leading down a passageway where seven jackets hung neatly on seven hooks, past a shelf where seven candles stood waiting to be lit.

Gingerly Lily opened the next door into a narrow bedroom with a sloping ceiling where seven beds stood in a row, all with white pillows and bright patchwork bedspreads, with a pair of soft slippers under each one.

"I'm tired!" Lily yawned at the sight of the seven comfy beds.

She walked down the row then sat on the furthest one and rubbed her eyes.

"'Ta-rum-tum-tum!'" Voices chanted a marching song far off in the forest. A lamp glowed yellow on the pure white snow.

"Really, *really* tired!" Lily repeated. She yawned again.

"Ta-rum-tum-tum!

Bang the big drum!"

The lamp glinted on the blades of seven small pickaxes. Seven weary miners made their way home.

"Perhaps I could just take a little nap," Lily said, lifting the bedspread and climbing into bed.

She was falling and floating, drifting off on a white cloud.

Silver light sparkled over her head. "Ta-rum-tum-tum!" Distant voices sang as she floated away.

"Uh-oh, here comes that bright silver light!" Pearl told Amber after they'd searched everywhere for Lily. "Is that part of the magic?"

"You'd better believe it!" Amber said. "It means Lily's on her way back."

Lily drifted through sparkling space. She ended with a whoosh, flat out on Amber's basement floor. "Wow, I'm sleepy!" she sighed.

Pearl rushed over to pull her up. "Wake up, Lily! What happened to you?"

Lily rubbed her eyes and opened them. "Give me a chance," she grumbled as the bright light faded.

"Wake up! Wake up!" Amber shook her.

"Uh. Where am I?"

"Lily, where have you been?" Amber demanded. She couldn't wait to hear. "Come on, Lily, wake up. You've got to tell Pearl and me all about it!"

Have you checked out...

www.dressingupdreams.net

It's the place to go for games, downloads, activities, sneak previews and lots of fun!

You'll find a special dressing-up game and lots of activities and fun things to do, as well as news on Dressing-Up Dreams and all your favourite characters.

Sign up to the newsletter at **www.dressingupdreams.net** to receive extra clothes for your Dressing-Up Dreams doll and the opportunity to enter special members only competitions.

What happens next...?
Log on to www.dressingupdreams.net for a sneak preview of my next adventure!

WIN A Dressing-Up Dreams GOODIE BAG!

CAN YOU SPOT THE TWO DIFFERENCES AND THE HIDDEN LETTER IN THESE TWO PICTURES OF LILY?

There is a spot-the-difference picture and hidden letter in the back of all four Dressing-Up Dreams books about Lily (look for the books with 5, 6, 7 or 8 on the spine). Hidden in one of the pictures above is a secret letter. Find all four letters and put them together to make a special Dressing-Up Dreams word, then send it to us. Each month, we will put the correct entries in a draw and one lucky winner will receive a magical Dressing-Up Dreams goodie bag including an exclusive Dressing-Up Dreams keyring!

Send your magical word, your name, age and address
on a postcard to: **Lily's Dressing-Up Dreams Competition**

UK Readers:	**Australian Readers:**	**New Zealand Readers:**
Hodder Children's Books	Hachette Children's Books	Hachette Livre NZ Ltd
338 Euston Road	Level 17/207 Kent Street	PO Box 100 749
London NW1 3BH	Sydney NSW 2000	North Shore City 0745
kidsmarketing@hodder.co.uk	childrens.books@hachette.com.au	childrensbooks@hachette.co.nz

Only one entry per child. Final draw: 30th August 2009
For full terms and conditions go to www.hachettechildrens.co.uk/terms

COLOURING FUN!

Carefully colour the Dressing-Up Dreams picture on the next page and then send it in to us.

Or you can draw your very own fairytale character. You might want to think about what they would wear or if they have special powers.

Each month, we will put the best entries on the website gallery and one lucky winner will receive a magical Dressing-Up Dreams goodie bag!

Send your drawing, your name, age and address on a postcard to:
Lily's Dressing-Up Dreams Competition

UK Readers:	**Australian Readers:**	**New Zealand Readers:**
Hodder Children's Books	Hachette Children's Books	Hachette Livre NZ Ltd
338 Euston Road	Level 17/207 Kent Street	PO Box 100 749
London NW1 3BH	Sydney NSW 2000	North Shore City 0745
kidsmarketing@hodder.co.uk	childrens.books@hachette.com.au	childrensbooks@hachette.co.nz

For full terms and conditions go to www.hachettechildrens.co.uk/terms